WALT DISNEY'S
LAMBERT
THE SHEEPISH LION

GROLIER
BOOK CLUB EDITION

It had been a busy night for Mr. Stork. He had delivered bundles of babies to many different places.

As the sun began to rise, Mr. Stork had only one bundle left to deliver. Even though he was very tired, he quickly flew to the sheep meadow.

When Mr. Stork arrived at the meadow, the sheep were still asleep.

"This must be the place," he said as he read the label on the bundle:

BABY LAMBS INSIDE
PLEASE DELIVER TO SHEEP MEADOW.

Mr. Stork prepared to
land. Then he flapped his
wings and swooped down.
The noise woke up all
the mother sheep.

The mother sheep recognized Mr. Stork instantly. They could hardly wait to see their new babies.

"Here you are, ladies," said Mr. Stork as five little lambs tumbled out of the sack.

Each little lamb ran on wobbly legs to its
mother. It was wonderful to cuddle against a warm,
woolly mother after the cold flight with Mr. Stork.

But something was wrong! There were six mother sheep and only five lambs! The last mother sheep began to cry. She felt very lonely.

"Now don't worry, Mrs. Sheep," Mr. Stork
said in a soothing voice. "I'm sure there were
six lambs in the sack." Mr. Stork shook the
sack, and out tumbled one more baby animal.

"Oh, dear, there must be some mistake," said Mr. Stork. He put on his eyeglasses and checked his order book.

"Aha!" Mr. Stork exclaimed a moment later. "It's Lambert, the lion cub, and he belongs somewhere else!"

But Lambert was already snuggling against
the mother sheep. She was smiling and Lambert
was purring just like the little kitten that he was.
The mother sheep did not look lonely anymore.

"Excuse me, Mrs. Sheep," said Mr. Stork.
"There has been a mistake! This baby is a
lion cub, and he belongs at the zoo."

Mrs. Sheep decided right there and then
that no one was going to take her new baby
away. She bent her head low and knocked
Mr. Stork high into the air.

"Silly old stork," said Mrs. Sheep
as she licked Lambert's little mane.
Lambert purred happily.

"Now run along and play with the other little lambs down in the meadow," said Mrs. Sheep. So off he went.

Lambert came to the top of a small hill.
He stopped to watch the lambs playing in
the grass. Although their brand-new legs
were still stiff and wobbly, they all jumped
and skipped around. They were having
lots of fun.

Then Lambert heard them call to one
another. *"BAAA, BAAA,"* the little
lambs called out.

Lambert wanted to play, too. So he opened his mouth to say *BAAA*. But the only sound that came out of his mouth was a great big *MEOW!*

When the other lambs heard Lambert's
meow, they started to laugh.

"What a strange lamb! He doesn't know
how to say BAAA!" the lambs exclaimed.

"His feet are too big!" said one
little lamb.

"And his tail is much too long!"
said another.

Poor Lambert! He felt very sad. The truth was that his feet *were* too big. His tail *was* too long. He was certainly the strangest-looking lamb in the meadow!

Lambert's mother came to comfort him.
"Don't worry about them, dear. Just watch
the lambs and do what they do. Then they'll
stop laughing at you."

Lambert felt much better and he went off
to play again.

But every time Lambert tried to leap like
a lamb, he tripped over his big feet…

…and landed on his head.

Lambert was good at playing the butting-heads game. But sometimes his head hurt from playing the game too often.

Strangest of all,
Lambert noticed that
he was bigger than
all the other sheep.

And it was true!
Every day Lambert was getting
bigger, and bigger, and bigger!

Lambert got so big that he hardly
even felt it when the young sheep played
the butting game.

And he never got angry when the sheep laughed at him.

Lambert just grinned a sheepish grin and pretended not to care.

But deep inside, Lambert *did* care.
He was tired of being butted.
He was tired of looking silly.
Most of all, he was tired
of being different.

One night, while the sheep were all sound asleep, Lambert heard a very strange noise.

It was the mean, hungry growl of a mean, hungry wolf! The wolf was creeping toward the sheep meadow. Lambert was terrified!

Lambert hid behind his mother.
He did not feel brave enough to
fight the mean, hungry wolf.

But the sheep were not brave, either. In fact, they were very sheepish sheep. When they heard the wolf getting closer and closer, they ran into the woods and hid behind trees…

…except for Lambert and his mother. Lambert's mother tried to protect him. But the wolf chased her away.

When Lambert heard his mother's cry for help, something snapped inside his head.

He forgot he was afraid.

He forgot he was a sheep.

He even forgot to *BAAAA!*

Instead, he opened his
mouth and ROARED!
Then he charged straight
at the wolf.

But Lambert did not forget everything he had learned in the sheep meadow. He lowered his big head and—POW! The wolf went flying right off the cliff.

After that, the wolf would
never bother the sheep in
the sheep meadow again.

Soon all the sheep came out of their hiding places. The sheep thought Lambert was a hero. They were glad that he was different. And they never made fun of him again.

"Did you hear my Lambert roar?" Lambert's mother asked the other mothers.

Lambert purred as they carried him along. It was a *mighty* purr—the purr of a very brave lion.